Jenna's Big Jump

Faythe Dyrud Thureen

Illustrated by

Elaine Sandeen

ATHENEUM 1993 NEW YORK

Maxwell Macmillan Canada
Toronto
Maxwell Macmillan International
New York Oxford Singapore Sydney

Atheneum
Macmillan Publishing Company
866 Third Avenue
New York, NY 10022

Maxwell Macmillan Canada, Inc.
1200 Eglinton Avenue East
Suite 200
Don Mills, Ontario M3C 3N1

Macmillan Publishing Company is part of the
Maxwell Communication Group of Companies.

First edition
Printed in the United States of America
10 9 8 7 6 5 4 3 2 1
The text of this book is set in 13 point Caslon.
The illustrations are rendered in pencil.
Book design by Kimberly M. Adlerman

Library of Congress Cataloging-in-Publication Data

Thureen, Faythe Dyrud.
    Jenna's big jump / Faythe Dyrud Thureen; illustrations by Elaine
Sandeen. — 1st ed.
        p.   cm.
    Summary: Jenna tries to stand up to the fourth grade bully and
plans an act of daring and bravery to prove herself to her mother.
    ISBN 0-689-31834-0
    [1. Courage—Fiction. 2. Schools—Fiction. 3. Bullies—Fiction.
4. Mothers and daughters—Fiction.] I. Sandeen, Elaine, ill.
II. Title.
PZ7.T42224Je 1993
[Fic]—dc20   92-23327

Dedicated to:

Soc Glasrud
Emily Rhoads Johnson
Rachel and Paul Thureen
Jeremy and Sarah Davis
Courtney Sheffield
Alex Joseph Wilborn

Acknowledgments

With appreciation to
Tom Clifford, President Emeritus
of the University of North Dakota,
who has supported and encouraged
the Writers Conference
in Children's Literature
since its beginning in 1980,
and to
Dr. Robert Johnson
and the Grand Forks
Orthopaedic Clinic staff,
for
reading X rays
and casting my arm

Contents

1

All Alone

Jenna Wexler was alone.

Alone in Marshall, Minnesota.

Alone in a new fourth-grade class of twenty-six kids.

Alone in her own kitchen, except for the boxes. Still-packed moving-day boxes covered the table, and empty ones were stacked high everywhere else.

Jenna sat at the counter, nibbling on a cookie. Only her thoughts kept her company.

It was Thursday, the day Mother had a late

afternoon class at the community college where she taught English. And Dad was still back in Thief River Falls. He couldn't leave his job at the bank until Halloween. Then his new job would be ready for him here in Marshall.

Mother and Dad had decided to move because their new jobs meant they had special places in this town. Jenna's special place was back in Thief River Falls with her best friend Kari, but no one had asked her opinion.

Jenna tried to concentrate on the homemade chocolate-chip oatmeal cookie, her favorite. But eating cookies wasn't the same here. In Thief River Falls, she always talked with Mother or Dad between bites.

She remembered telling them about how she and Kari pretended they were Ramona Quimby and her sister Beezus. They argued so loudly that they felt like real sisters. Dad had laughed and said it was a good thing she was an only child.

He was wrong. If she had brothers and sisters, they would be here to stick up for her when that bully chased her on the school playground. And she wouldn't be alone right now.

Jenna slid off the stool. She picked up the big picture lying on the kitchen desk, waiting to be hung. How lucky Mother had been to have ten brothers and sisters! Jenna propped the picture against the wall and sat down.

She loved to look at the scene. Her aunt Helene had painted the family of seven boys and four girls and their mother and father, and Grandpa and Grandma Paulsen. In the background, leafy branches reached over the farmhouse, inviting climbers.

The yard was alive with activity. Barefoot Uncle Keith rolled a huge truck tire past pink hollyhocks, and chickens scattered. Philip helped Grandpa Paulsen repair the tractor. Jonathan and Clifford held bottles to feed woolly black lambs. David scratched the head of a goat balancing on a post. Two little girls—Jenna knew they were her aunts Gracia and Rachel—held hands and raced with a black and white dog. Harlan carried pails of fresh milk from the barn. A bright orange cat eyed the milk hungrily from her perch on the porch steps. On the porch, Helene and Grandma Paulsen guided a bed sheet through the washing machine wringers.

I know for sure what I'd be doing if I were there, thought Jenna. I'd be petting that cat. How I wish I could snatch the cat out of the picture and name her Flame!

In the picture, Mother was not much older than Jenna. But she was the big sister, swinging a laughing Baby Dwight high into a tree on a tire swing.

With all those people and animals in her family, Mother didn't have any idea what it meant to be lonely. So she couldn't really understand Jenna's sad feelings.

Jenna left the picture and pulled Beverly Cleary's *Ramona, Forever* out of her schoolbag. She started to read, but it only made her feel worse. Ramona already had a sister, and now her mother was going to have another baby. And Ramona wasn't even excited about it. The words Jenna was reading began to blur together. She shut the book and rubbed her wet eyes. If only she could trade places with Ramona.

Advice

The sound of a key rattling in the lock startled Jenna. The door opened and Mother appeared carrying a grocery bag. "Hi, honey! How's my latchkey kid?"

"How do you think I am?" Though Jenna was relieved to see Mother, she felt angry at her at the same time.

Mother set the bag on the counter and pulled out a frozen lasagna. "When I get the boxes unpacked and everything in its place, you'll forget you aren't back in Thief River Falls."

"I wish," Jenna sighed.

"What is that supposed to mean?" Mother put the lasagna in the microwave and gave Jenna a shoulder squeeze.

"I don't think this will ever feel like my real home."

Mother poured two glasses of milk and sat down next to Jenna. "You'll adjust. It's only been a week."

"*Only.* It seems like a year to me." Jenna took a long drink of milk. "Every day is worse. I still don't have any friends, and today Buzz chased me with a rubber snake."

A faraway look and a slight smile appeared on Mother's face.

"Mom!" Jenna felt like her mother hadn't understood what she said. "It wasn't funny at all."

"I'm sorry, Jenna. I was just thinking about how lucky Buzz is that he wasn't picking on me when I was your age."

"Why? What would you have done?"

Mother laughed. "That wouldn't help you much now. What you need to know is what *you* should do. Whatever you do, don't run when someone runs after you. Just ignore that boy. He'll soon get tired of picking on you." Mother patted Jenna's hand and got up.

"Sounds easy. But tell me what you did. I know you're thinking about something that happened when you were little." Jenna loved Mother's stories.

"Right now, it's time for you to set the table and for me to toss a salad," Mother said. "I have an idea. Tomorrow night I'll fix the kind of supper we used to have when I was a child. And we'll have a Friday night story time to celebrate the completion of a week of school for both of us."

"All right," Jenna agreed. "At least I have *something* to look forward to."

Jenna Has a Disease

The next morning, Jenna hurried into the school building. She didn't want to risk running into Buzz on the playground.

"Good morning, Jenna." Mr. Larson finished writing his thought for the day on the board and smiled at her. "This is your last day as the new kid in class. Enjoy it." He sat down at his desk.

Jenna wondered what he meant.

She read the sentence on the board, "A friend in need is a friend indeed." Oh, Kari, she thought. Where are you when I need you most?

If only you could be here to play with me at noon hour.

During classes Jenna felt almost comfortable. The reading book was the same one Kari was using. When they talked on the phone, she and Kari had decided to do their first book report on *Ramona, Forever.* So it was easy for Jenna to pretend she was back in Thief River Falls.

In social studies, Mr. Larson had each of the students go to the map to find a different state. When it was Jenna's turn, she pointed out Delaware and quickly returned to her desk.

"Buzz. Please find Florida," Mr. Larson directed.

Buzz went to the map, picked up the pointer on the blackboard ledge, and waved it with a flourish above Florida. On its way down, the pointer caught the pull ring. The map rolled up with a snap and fell to the floor. Buzz looked startled. Then he started to laugh. He stopped when no one else joined in. The class was quiet, waiting.

Mr. Larson's voice was stern. "Pick up the map and see me after lunch."

A feeling of relief washed over Jenna. Buzz

would surely have to stay in all noon hour to write sentences.

After lunch, Jenna sat in a swing and watched the other kids play. Julie and Brenda teeter-tottered together, as usual. They reminded her of Kari and herself. Some of the girls and boys were playing dodgeball. All of them seemed to know where they belonged. They acted like Jenna was invisible, but she didn't care much. She was just glad Buzz wasn't there to chase her.

Suddenly Jenna noticed Julie and Brenda walking toward her. "Come on, Jenna. Let's go and play dodge with the others," Julie invited.

It was the first time anyone had asked her to play. Jenna felt nervous, but stood up to follow them.

Just then, a loud voice chanted, "Jenna, Jenna, Jenna. Belongs in a penna!" And Buzz came running toward her.

Jenna froze. She felt like running away but remembered what Mother had said.

Buzz stopped too. He turned to Julie and Brenda. "Don't come any closer, ladies. I have been ordered to place this creature in new-kid quarantine. Who knows what deadly disease she brings to Marshall?" Then he started to chant again, "Jenna, Jenna, Jenna. Belongs in a penna." He kept on until the two girls walked away. Then he ran off.

Jenna blinked back tears. No one would ever want to be her friend now.

The whistle blew, and she walked back to her classroom alone.

The afternoon was long. Jenna didn't dare to look up from her books and papers. She wondered how many of the others had heard Buzz and if they believed that she had a disease.

Just before school was out, Mr. Larson read the thought for the day, " 'A friend in need is a friend indeed.' I want you to take special note of this, class. On Monday we will have a new student, whom I want you to be prepared to welcome."

"Is it a boy or a girl?" someone asked.

"I don't know," said Mr. Larson. "There are several children in the family, and one of them will be in fourth grade."

"It doesn't really matter," Buzz said. "If it's a boy, I'll see that he gets a great welcome."

Buzz held up a fist. "If it's a girl, I'll quarantine her with Jenna so no one else gets their disease."

Jenna could feel Buzz's words paint her face red for the whole class to stare at. As soon as the bell rang, she rushed out of the classroom. All she wanted to do was get home to Mother's story and never come back to school again.

A Feast

"**S**uppertime." Mother's voice interrupted Jenna's game of charades with Kari.

Reluctantly, Jenna rubbed her eyes open. She saw encyclopedias stacked in front of an empty bookcase. "Oh no," she groaned. She wasn't in Thief River Falls at all. It had only been another dream. The ache of loneliness was still deep in her stomach. She slowly got up from the couch. Her feet dragged to the kitchen.

"I thought I'd be enjoying my olden-days meal by myself," said Mother. Jenna walked into Mother's hug. "You slept for almost three hours. Did you work that hard in school today?"

Jenna shivered. She pushed herself away. "I don't even want to think about school." She looked at the bare counter. "Where's the food?"

Mother gestured toward the table.

Jenna blinked. The boxes were gone, and so were the chairs. A tall, metal can covered with a little pillow stood by the table. Next to it was a wooden carton standing on end.

"The crate is for you," Mother said, matter-of-factly. "I'll sit on the eight-gallon milk can."

Jenna sat down carefully. The crate opened in front for her legs. "It's a little wobbly," she said.

"Yes, it would crash under me for sure," said Mother. "That's why I'm using this strong can. It's just like the one my mother sat on."

"But why didn't you use regular chairs when you were little?" asked Jenna.

"For one thing, we didn't have enough to go around, and I'm afraid we were quite hard on the ones we did have. Spindles on chair backs didn't last long among our rambunctious crew.

So most of us had backless chairs or crates like yours. Only my father had a chair with a back."

Jenna wiggled into a comfortable position on the crate and examined the unusual place settings. "I suppose you ate out of pie tins and drank from soup cans like these, so they wouldn't break."

Mother laughed and nodded. "Guaranteed childproof. By the way, don't worry about cutting your mouth on the can seam. That happened to me a few times, so I've checked ours carefully."

Jenna examined her drinking can suspiciously. "If you hadn't told me, I wouldn't have known there was anything to worry about." She looked around for the food. "Well? I'm getting hungry. What's on the menu besides margarine and honey."

Mother dramatically uncovered a steaming kettle. "Presenting the main course." She spooned a gray-brown mush onto each plate.

"Am I supposed to eat that?" Jenna sniffed the suspicious-looking glob. "What is it?"

"It's ground wheat cereal. Your grandfather,

who used to grind the wheat himself, called it porridge for royalty." Mother dabbed some margarine in the center of her cereal, then spooned honey over all. "Now serve yourself, Princess."

Jenna copied Mother, dipping a spoonful of mush into the pool of melting margarine. She moved it around her mouth cautiously then decided it was safe to swallow. There was nothing great about the stuff. Without honey, she was sure it would be tasteless.

Mother was obviously enjoying it. "Mmm! Isn't it the best food you've ever had?"

Jenna made a face at Mother. "Sure. Almost as good as pizza." She coated a spoonful of mush with lots of margarine then balanced the spoon daintily between her fingers. "But the best part is the atmosphere." She stuck her nose in the air and spoke in a sophisticated voice, the way she did when she and Kari pretended they were dining in a fancy restaurant. "The china is elegant and isn't this fine furniture the ultimate in comfort!" They laughed together, and Jenna felt good.

"Actually, this 'chair' would be better off back

home in the barn with the cows." Mother poured milk and tried to get comfortable.

For dessert, they peeled and sectioned oranges. "Just like the good old days." Mother laughed when she said it, as though it were a joke.

But Jenna liked this old-fashioned world and was eager to stay. "I'm ready for the story," she said hurriedly when Mother got up from the table.

"All right. Let's find a more comfortable spot." Mother picked up the pie tins and carried them to the sink. "You can throw the cans in the trash, Jenna. I think we'll drink from glasses next time."

Toughkid

Jenna snuggled next to Mother on the couch. "Is it an exciting story?"

"It was when I lived it, about . . ." She squinted her eyes. "Let's see, I'm forty four years old now, and I was six then."

"Thirty-eight years ago," said Jenna. "Wow! That's so long ago I'm surprised you can even remember."

"My brothers have never let me forget."

"Then it must have been something awful. Hurry and tell it!"

Mother began. "The May morning was warm and sunny. A mountain of white clouds decorated the sky, but one dark cloud floated some distance from the others."

"You can't remember that," Jenna interrupted.

"You're right. That part is made up, but it gives you a clue to something in the story. What do you think the dark cloud could indicate?"

"Maybe that it's going to rain. But I think you're forgetting this is not a college English class."

Mother laughed. "On with the story."

It was a day I had been waiting for for a long time. This was the first time I would visit school with my big brothers. We didn't have kindergarten, so I would start first grade the next fall.

Harlan, Philip, and Keith walked down the road to meet the school bus. I ran.

When the bus stopped, I quickly climbed on ahead of the others. Keith and I sat together. I would be visiting first grade with him.

"Where is he?" I asked immediately.

Keith frowned, "Who are you talking about?"

"You know, George Sigdahl."

"Shh." Keith looked around nervously. "Don't let *him* hear you!"

"Tell me where he is," I whispered.

"Across the aisle and two seats ahead. And don't stare. If he notices you, you're in for trouble."

But I did stare. So that was *the* George Sigdahl I had heard so much about. I was surprised. This wasn't the tough-looking, muscular kid I had expected. This blond boy was only slightly larger than I and, from the back, looked harmless. The only thing that made him stand out from the others were the rips in the seams of his shirtsleeves.

Suddenly, George's arm shot out and hurled a wad of paper toward the front of the bus. The wad bounced off the windshield and fell to the floor.

The bus pulled off to the side of the road, and the driver stood up. His face was as red as a rooster's comb.

"Who is responsible for this?" he shouted. He waved the paper ball in the air and looked straight at George.

"I didn't do it!" George's voice sounded as angry as the bus driver's. "Just ask Wally. He's been sitting by me the whole time."

Wally shook his head. "I didn't see nothing."

I couldn't believe my ears. My hand shot up. Keith pulled it down.

The bus driver glanced our way, then sat down and started driving.

"What are you thinking of!" Keith scolded. "If you tattle on him, it'll be the end of both of us."

My brothers had told me about braids George had pulled, windows he had broken, and kids he had tripped and punched. He had even made a teacher cry. "Why doesn't anybody ever stop him?" I whispered.

"Everybody's scared of him," Keith whispered back.

"I'm not," I said. "He isn't even as big as you, and sometimes *I* can beat up on you."

"Shush! You'd better not say that in school." Keith looked worried.

"I won't. But I'll *do* what I want." And I knew just what I was going to do.

When the bus stopped at school, I was one of the first ones off, even before George. I had a job to do and nothing was going to stop me.

"Hurry up!" George shoved the girl ahead of him and stepped off the bus.

I was waiting for him. I blocked his path and said, "I saw you throw that spitball."

George stepped back in surprise. "Who do you think you are?"

"I'm Marie Paulsen, and I don't like the bad things you do."

"I don't care what you like. I'm tough, and you'd better get out of my way, or you'll be sorry."

But I didn't budge. "I'm not scared of you, and I'm going to stand here till you tell the bus driver it was you."

"Marie!" I heard my big brother Harlan's urgent voice. "Come here."

I looked up and saw a crowd of kids watching and listening. Just then, I felt the impact of George's foot against my shin. He turned to run, but I grabbed his arm.

If no one else would stop him, I had to. I quickly threw him to the grass, face down. Then I sat on his back and pinned his hands to the ground. Keith couldn't get up from that hold, and I hoped George wouldn't either.

He wriggled and struggled. Then he shouted, "Let me go!" When that didn't work, he yelled, *"Help!"*

Suddenly I became aware of the bus driver standing over us. "What's going on here?" he asked.

"George has something to tell you," I said.

"Okay, I'll tell." George tried to pull his hands out from under mine. "But you let me go first."

"Oh no!" I was going to make sure he didn't get away. "You tell him first."

"I threw the paper," George mumbled.

I released his hands and got up.

The bus driver walked George toward the school.

I scanned the crowd, looking for Keith.

Somebody called out, "Yeah, Toughkid!" Others clapped and cheered.

Keith stepped forward and took my hand to lead me to first grade. He didn't say anything, but I knew he was proud of me.

Jenna looked at Mother in awe, trying to see the little Marie in the story. "You were so brave!"

Mother laughed and gave Jenna a hug. "Think brave thoughts yourself and get to bed."

Jenna lay in bed trying to pretend that she was Marie. But George became Buzz, and she ran away from him. She shivered and pulled the covers over her head trying to hide from Buzz and lock out Marshall School. It didn't work. The aching fear gnawed in her stomach. A very big, black cloud grew in the sky, and Jenna wasn't brave enough to make it go away. Why couldn't she be like Mother?

The New Student

Jenna and Kari talked on the phone for a long time Saturday. They were both studying Hawaii in social studies, so they planned a winter trip to Maui beach. They would sway gracefully doing the hula, surf on gentle waves, and savor chunks of juicy pineapple. Maybe they would stay there and never go to school again.

On Sunday, Jenna tried to persuade Mother to let her get a kitten. It would be orange and white and fluffy, and its name would be *Amie*, which is the French word for friend. Jenna already had a blanket-lined basket waiting in her bedroom.

But Mother wasn't in a hurry to get a kitten. "Maybe after I'm through unpacking, and your father is home," she said. She didn't seem to realize that Jenna needed a kitten desperately. Now.

Monday came too soon. When Jenna got to school, she felt like turning around and running back home again. Her legs were weak and trembly when she walked into the classroom.

"Our new student is Kate Bradner," Mr. Larson announced.

"I was hoping it would be a boy," Buzz said. "We already have too many new girls." He pointed at Jenna.

Before Jenna could even look down, she heard a new voice.

"It looks to me like there's one boy too many in this class." Jenna looked in surprise at the new girl. She had a determined set to her jaw and was looking straight at Buzz.

Jenna forgot about herself for a moment and

had a worried feeling for the girl. Obviously Kate didn't realize how much trouble Buzz could cause for her.

Mr. Larson looked surprised too. "All right, let's settle down and take out our math books," he said.

Kate was the first one to put her math paper on the teacher's desk. When she turned around, Buzz jumped up and hurried forward. He met her in the aisle and bumped into her. Jenna watched tensely as Kate tried to walk around Buzz, but he blocked her way. With a quick shove, she pushed him aside and returned to her desk.

Yes! Two points for Kate, thought Jenna. But what would happen at noon on the playground? Would Buzz try to get back at Kate, or would he keep on bothering Jenna?

Jenna ate lunch slowly to take up as much playtime as possible. When she got to the play-ground, she looked around and immediately spotted Buzz standing by the swings. Jenna moved toward the dodgeball game, hoping Buzz wouldn't see her.

Kate was playing dodge. Jenna could tell by

the way she threw the ball hard and straight and by her high leaps that she was a good player. But how had she gotten into the game so fast on her first day in Marshall? Jenna hadn't dared to barge in without being asked. She glanced at Buzz and was relieved that his back was to her.

Then she heard his voice, "Baby Tommy wants his mommy. Baby Tommy wants his mommy."

Jenna shuddered at the sound. She looked more closely. Buzz was turning a swing in circles. The chains were twisted almost to the top. He dropped the swing and stepped back. Jenna could see a younger boy turning in the swing. She saw the look of terror on his face. The swing spun faster as it untwisted, and the boy started to whimper. But Buzz kept on chanting, "Baby Tommy wants his mommy."

Suddenly, Kate appeared, stopped the swing, and helped the boy out. She put her arms around his shoulders to steady him. She looked up at Buzz in disdain. "Get out of here and never come near my brother again!" she ordered. Then she turned back to the boy and talked softly.

Buzz ran toward the school and disappeared around a corner.

Kate wiped her brother's tears with her fingers. Jenna touched the Kleenex packet in her pocket and wanted to give it to Kate. Her feet seemed to make the decision. She ran over to the swings and handed the Kleenex to Kate.

Kate took out a tissue and dabbed the boy's face. "It'll be okay now, Tommy."

The boy shook his head, "My school name isn't Tommy anymore. It's Tom."

Jenna gave him a pat on the back. "Hang in there, Tom. Now, go and find some other second-graders." He walked away slowly.

"Thank you." Kate handed Jenna the Kleenex packet and ran back to the dodgeball game.

Jenna sat down on a swing. While she waited for the whistle to blow, she thought about Kate. She liked the way Kate seemed so sure of herself.

Buzz Off

The next day, for the first time since she came to Marshall, Jenna didn't dread going to school. If Buzz picked on her, she would try to pretend it didn't bother her. But it wasn't only that. She wondered what Kate would do today.

Kate was already in the classroom, standing by the teacher's desk. Mr. Larson was showing her what the class had covered in reading. "And if you have any questions, I'm sure Jenna would be glad to help you. She's a good reader, and she knows what it's like to be new in Marshall."

Jenna smiled shyly when Kate greeted her with a wave. Kate didn't look like the kind of person who would need help with anything, but Jenna was happy for the excuse to be with her.

When Jenna got to the playground at noon, Kate was standing on a swing, pumping high in the air. Without looking for Buzz, Jenna ran to the swings and took the one next to Kate. She sat sideways and watched Kate soar into the sky, black hair waving behind her. Her body stretched out even with the top bar, then relaxed momentarily, before swinging to earth again.

Watching Kate made Jenna feel free and happy and brave. Then a terrible sound interrupted her feelings.

"Jenna, Jenna, Jenna. Belongs in a penna." Buzz was standing a short distance in front of her. "Look out, Kate!" Buzz called. "Jenna has a disease."

"Oh no!" Jenna hoped Kate wouldn't hear and walk away like Brenda and Julie.

Just then, an empty swing jingled next to Jenna, and Kate flew through the air. She landed easily on both feet in front of Buzz. Buzz stumbled backward.

Jenna felt a sudden surge of courage. She jumped off the swing and shouted, "Buzz off!" To her surprise, he did. He ran away without looking back.

Jenna and Kate laughed together. Then they grabbed swings and slid into the black seats again.

"You looked like a flying trapeze artist," Jenna said.

"Someday I will fly. I'm going to be a pilot." Kate twisted her swing around Jenna's swing chains. "Now you're my copilot." They twirled around together, laughing, then untwisted with a jerk.

"You really scared Buzz," Jenna said.

"You're the one that sent him buzzing off," said Kate.

"And that's what you have to do with people like him." Kate sat still and looked serious. "I told my dad what he did to Tommy, and he thinks maybe someone else is hurting Buzz. But he also says that's no excuse for Buzz to be cruel to others."

Jenna hadn't even thought about Buzz's feelings.

"I didn't play dodge today, because I wanted to talk to you," Kate continued. "I was wondering if you would like to be my friend. The other kids already have their best friends, and I know we'd have fun together."

It seemed so easy for Kate to say her thoughts out loud. It made Jenna feel like she didn't have to hide her own feelings. "I was hoping you'd be my friend," Jenna said. "I could tell you about the first stories in our reader, and maybe you would teach me to swing like that."

"Oh, I know something even more fun." Kate looked excited. "We just moved to a farm, and there's a barn, and I want to show you a surprise in the hayloft. When can you come to my house?"

Jenna felt excited too. "If you have animals, I'd like to go right now."

"We do! We have two cats named Panther and Dusty and a dog named Seetuk. Can you come tomorrow?"

Jenna knew Mother wouldn't let her go to a strange place when she didn't know the people. "Maybe not tomorrow. My mother will have to talk to yours first."

"I know. My parents are like that too. We don't have a phone yet, but my mom could call yours from the hospital where she works."

Jenna promised to write down her home phone number and Mother's at the college. She felt great! This was almost as good as going to visit Kari.

Jenna got home only fifteen minutes before Mother, but it seemed like hours. She was so excited that she started to talk the minute her mother stepped inside. "Kate swings higher than anybody and she's my new friend and she has cats and a dog and we scared Buzz away and . . ."

"Stop!" Mother raised her palm. "You're forgetting the punctuation."

"Please, Mom. May I go to Kate's farm on Thursday, instead of staying here alone? Her mother will call you."

"We'll see." Mother smiled and squeezed Jenna's hand. "It's been a long time since I've seen you so happy."

"It's because I like my assignment. Mr. Larson said I'm supposed to help Kate adjust to Marshall."

Mother laughed. "If it's an assignment, I suppose I'll have to let you go."

Jenna reached up and gave Mother a big hug.

Kate's House

On Thursday morning, Jenna ate her pancakes fast. This was the day she was going to ride the school bus to Kate's farm.

"I told Mrs. Bradner I'd be there to pick you up as soon after class as possible." Mother handed Jenna her schoolbag. "Be polite and don't do anything dangerous."

"Don't be in any rush to pick me up. I'll be just fine." Jenna waved at Mother and hurried out the door.

At noon, Jenna and Kate teeter-tottered

together. "I can't wait to see what's in your barn," Jenna said.

"Well, there aren't any animals . . . yet. The surprise is in the hayloft." Kate stopped teetering. "Come on, let's go play dodge."

The girls were put on different teams. Jenna felt good about being part of the group. And Kate didn't throw the ball at her at first, so she got to play for a while before a fast ball hit her.

The school day was finally over. Jenna followed Kate down the aisle of the bus to a seat where a little girl with black hair and happy eyes like Kate's was sitting. Kate patted her arm. "Hi, Mara. Can you make room for two today?"

The girl smiled and moved over. "Hi, Kate and Jenna."

Jenna was surprised that Mara already knew her name.

"Mara's in afternoon kindergarten," Kate said. Then she gestured to Jenna. "You get in first. I have to sit on the outside, just in case Tommy needs me."

Jenna sat comfortably squished between the two sisters. She didn't have to wonder long what Kate meant.

Suddenly Buzz hurdled down the aisle. He pointed at Jenna and yelled, "Contaminated! This bus is contaminated." Then he stumbled to the backseat and sat down by himself.

Kate laughed. "He's the one who's contaminated. Nobody will even sit by him."

Jenna forced a smile. "I'm glad you think he's funny. He still scares me."

"He's more pitiful than funny," Kate said. "Dad wants me to watch so he doesn't bother Tommy. He says sometimes when big guys are mean to little kids, the little kids take it out on kids that are smaller than they are. And we don't want Tommy to get to be like Buzz."

Jenna saw Tommy sitting with another boy.

"He doesn't want us to sit near him," Kate said. "He wants to look like a big boy. But he knows I'm here."

"I wish I had sisters and brothers," Jenna said.

"It's nice most of the time," Mara said.

"When isn't it nice?" Jenna asked.

"When Kate's bossy." Mara giggled and snuggled against Jenna for protection from Kate, who was making a monster face.

"Guess who doesn't get to play in the hayloft today?" Kate threatened.

"I take back what I said," Mara said quickly.

"But I still remember," Kate responded.

Mara reached across Jenna and rubbed her sister's head. "There. Now I erased it from your brain."

"You're just lucky Jenna is between us." Kate laughed. "All right. I want you to show her what you can do anyway."

"I can hardly wait to see what's so much fun in that barn," Jenna said.

"You'll soon find out," Mara said, as the bus slowed down. "Here we are."

Jenna looked out the window and saw a girl smaller than Mara, a white dog, and two cats waiting. Jenna felt like a celebrity being met by a welcoming committee.

When she stepped off the bus, the little girl called, "Hi, Jenna." Ignoring the others, she grabbed Jenna's hand.

"I'm Molly and I waited for you all day and I'm four years old."

Jenna squeezed the small, warm hand. "Who are your pets?"

Molly pointed to the white Siberian husky with milky blue eyes. "That's Seetuk. The black cat is Panther. And the one that's gray and white and orange is Dusty."

"Panther is my cat," Tommy said. "She's fierce." He pushed out his chest like a track star and sprinted toward the house.

"Yes, can't you just hear her growl." Kate stroked the purring Panther.

White paint was peeling off the house, and screens were torn. Jenna wondered what it would be like inside. She sniffed. It smelled wonderful! Mara led her into the kitchen where four loaves of fresh bread were lined up on racks in the middle of a table.

"Anybody hungry?" A man with no hair on top, a bushy gray fringe covering his ears, and a reddish beard smiled at Jenna. He reminded her of Dusty, the calico cat, but his eyes looked like Kate's and Mara's.

"Hi." Jenna felt kind of shy and didn't know what else to say. But she didn't have to say anything, because the others talked for her.

"Yes! Fresh bread."

"Where's the strawberry jam?"

"I want milk with mine."

Tommy picked up a loaf and opened his mouth wide. "I could eat this whole thing."

"You can sit by me, Jenna." Molly pointed to a strange-looking, very narrow bench.

Jenna slid onto it and balanced carefully.

"Our makeshift benches are really saw-horses," Mr. Bradner explained. "If you look under the slab of wood that serves as a table, you'll see that it's propped up with sawhorses too. I'll get something more comfortable made next week." He sliced a loaf of bread and arranged slices on a platter.

Kate set out milk, butter, and jam. Jenna almost expected Kate to put out tin cans to drink from, but she passed around mugs. Kate poured milk for Molly, and the others helped themselves.

"This is the best bread you've ever made, Daddy." Mara closed her eyes and made a funny, happy face.

"You have a strawberry mustache, Mara," Tommy laughed.

"And you have a buttery nose, Tommy." Molly pointed at him.

He quickly wiped his nose with the back of his hand, and retorted, "It isn't polite to talk to your elders like that, Molly."

Kate turned to Jenna. "Now you see what it's like to have a brother and sisters."

Jenna just laughed. It didn't look bad to her.

"Come and see our bedroom." Molly jumped off the bench and took Jenna's hand again. Mara followed.

Three sleeping bags were lined up on the floor. Mara and Molly jumped onto theirs.

"This one is Kate's." Mara patted the middle bag. She sleeps here to keep Molly and me from fighting.

"And here are my clothes." Molly opened a colorful trunk at the head of her sleeping bag.

Mara sat down on her trunk. "These are our chairs too. Here, you can sit on Kate's."

Jenna sat down and smiled at the happy girls. "You can pretend you're camping together. I wish I had somebody to share my room with."

Kate appeared in the doorway. "Just bring your sleeping bag. You can help protect me from these pests."

"But Jenna likes *us* too, Kate," Molly said.

Kate ignored her. "We sold all our furniture when we moved here. Dad said it was easier and cheaper to move that way. He's staying home to fix up the house and build some furniture before winter, while Mom works. During the winter, she'll stay home and Dad will go to work in a counseling office. He helps people with problems."

"And I stay home to help," Molly said.

"Good," Kate said. "Then you can stay in the house and help Dad when we go to the barn to play."

"Oh no!" Molly squealed and ran out of the bedroom with Mara.

The Hayloft

enna followed Kate through a side door of the barn into a large loft. Except for a mound of hay on one side, it was empty. Rafters held up the barn roof high above Jenna and Kate.

Tommy was already in the loft. Jenna watched him hustle up a ladder attached to a wall across from the door where she stood. When he reached the top of the ladder, he threw himself over a ledge onto a floor.

"That's the upstairs," Kate explained.

"I'm going first," Tommy called. "Throw me the rope."

Kate hurried toward a rope dangling in the pile of hay. She grabbed it, swung it back and forth a couple of times, then flung it toward the wall.

Jenna held her breath as she watched Tommy lean forward over the open loft. He caught the rope easily. She wondered what was going to happen next.

A moment later, Tommy's lithe body swung through the air. Jenna's stomach dropped to her toes. Tommy bounced on the hay, jumped to his feet, and raised his arms above his head. "Good one," he shouted happily.

Jenna was relieved to see that he was all right. She could hardly believe this was the same Tommy she had seen crying on the school swings.

"Nice going, Tom!" Kate praised him.

Jenna nodded, "I thought we were going to have to pick you up."

Tommy looked proud. "I surprised you, didn't I? Wait till next time. I'll swing twice."

"It's my turn first," Mara called from upstairs. "Throw me the rope."

Mara looked so small. And there was a deep drop between her and the hay. It looked very dangerous. "Are you going to let her do it?" Jenna felt weak as she watched Tommy hurl the rope toward his younger sister.

"She just took her first swing the day before yesterday, but she's already good at it," Kate said. "Dad helped her practice."

Mara looked at Jenna to make sure she was watching, then swung out with a big smile on her face. She was still smiling when she bounced out of the hay pile. "It's so much fun, Jenna! Just wait till your turn."

Jenna's relief mixed with apprehension. She turned to Kate. "I can't do that!"

Kate laughed. "Not until you've practiced for a while. I'll take my turn, then I'll show you how." She flew through the air and landed on her feet as gracefully as she had coming off the school swing.

"It looks like so much fun, but I don't feel like I'll ever dare," Jenna said.

"That's what I thought last week," Tommy

said. "Now see what I can do." He grabbed the rope and wrapped his legs around it as he swung out. Instead of dropping into the hay, he swung back. When he reached the upstairs floor, he kicked the ledge, snapped out again over the open space, and finally dropped into the hay. He was panting for breath when he got up. "That's a long ride," he gasped. "But it gets easier every time."

"You do great," Kate said. "It's still hard for *me* the second time around. I feel like my hands are going to slip before I reach the hay." She grabbed the rope and tied a couple of big knots in the bottom.

"That's for you and me to practice," Molly said.

Jenna was amazed. "*You* aren't going to do this too, are you?"

Molly took the rope Kate handed her. "Daddy says I can't swing from the top till I'm five like Mara. But I'm going to practice, so I can be as good as Tommy."

Tommy looked pleased. He smiled at his little sister and said, "You might even be better."

Molly and Tommy walked over to the ladder

wall with the rope. Tommy held the bottom of the rope while Molly climbed three rungs of the ladder. Molly positioned her feet on the knot and held on tightly.

"Go!" she called out and sailed toward the hay. Instead of dropping, she swung back and kicked the wall to go again. When she had gone back and forth a few times, she dropped the short distance into the hay. She rolled giggling down the little haystack and got to her feet.

"Now I'll tell *you* how." Molly gave Jenna the rope. "Don't worry. It isn't hard." She walked to the ladder with Jenna. "Be sure to let go the first time."

"That's right," Kate said. "Drop into the hay the first time so you get the feel of it. After that you can start going back and forth like Molly."

Jenna climbed up two rungs. "I'm scared, but I'm going to do it," she said. After all, she thought, if Molly can do it, so can I. Kate held the rope while Jenna got on. As soon as her feet were on the knot, the rope took off. The next thing she knew, she was dropping into the hay. Her legs trembled as she stood up, but she felt happy.

"The first time is always the hardest," Kate said. "From now on you just have to practice until you get the feel of it. Then I'll take the knots out so your arms can get strong enough for the big swing. Don't be in any hurry, though. It'll take a few days before you're ready to go from the top. We don't take any chances."

Jenna rested and watched the others go through their routines again. It looked so easy and like such fun. She was beginning to get excited and wondered how long it would take before she'd be ready.

"Now Jenna can practice as much as she likes," Kate announced.

Soon Jenna felt comfortable swinging back and forth many times before letting go. She loved the feeling of flying through the air and falling into the hay. After she had practiced for a while, Kate untied the knots and had Jenna climb another step up before swinging out. Jenna's hands burned as they slid on the rope, but she managed to hang on until she reached the hay.

"Isn't it fun!" Kate said. "Next time you can

practice from even higher rungs of the ladder, so you get used to dropping at the right time."

Jenna rubbed her sore hands together.

"Your hands get stronger from practice too," Kate said.

Mara showed Jenna her palms. "My blisters are healing now."

"If you keep this up, Jenna, you'll have a few of those too," Kate said.

"Well, I'm not going to quit." Jenna was filled with a determination that was bigger than her fear. She knew she was going to swing from the top . . . very soon.

"Jenna, your mother is here." Tommy stood looking out the door.

"Let's go!" Jenna said. "I don't want Mom to see this until I can swing all the way. I want to surprise her."

The four ran toward the house together, trying not to stumble over Seetuk, who wove among the maze of legs.

"Two mothers are here," Molly said.

Mrs. Bradner sat on a sawhorse, elbows on the table and her chin propped on her hands. She looked tired.

Jenna's mother stood next to the table. Jenna wondered if she was afraid to sit down. The sawhorse was certainly as comfortable as that milk can Mother had used as a chair.

After everyone was introduced, Mother said to Jenna, "We have to go home now. But Kate's parents have agreed to let her come home with you tomorrow."

The two girls clapped their hands.

"Now I get to see your house," Kate said.

"It isn't as much fun as your farm," Jenna said. "But you'll get to hear Mom's Friday story."

Mr. Bradner handed Mother a brown bag. "Here's a loaf of bread, just in case Kate is ravenously hungry tomorrow."

"Thanks," Mother said. "It smells wonderful."

Kate walked to the car with Jenna.

"I need your help with something in my basement," Jenna whispered.

Kate nodded. "Okay. I can't wait!"

Jenna jumped into the car, buckled her seat belt, and waved to Kate. Then she turned to Mother. "That's the most fun I've ever had!

56

When I get big, I'm going to have at least two children."

"Wonderful!" Mother said. "Then I'll always have somebody to listen to my stories."

"They'll like your stories," Jenna said. But to herself she said, I'm going to have some exciting stories of my own to tell.

A Fall

After school the next day, Kate walked home with Jenna. Mother was already there with a snack waiting for them on the counter.

The girls jumped onto the stools and looked curiously at their plates. On each was a slice of bread. "What's this?" Jenna asked. To her surprise, Mother opened a carton of half-and-half cream. They never used cream at their house. Her parents said it was loaded with cholesterol. This must be a very special occasion.

Mother poured cream on her own bread until

the slice was soaked. She passed the carton to Kate, then shook a generous spoonful of brown sugar on top of her slice. "Cream on bread," she announced, almost reverently. While Jenna and Kate watched, she cut a brown and white square and slid her fork under it. As she gently placed the morsel in her mouth, a look of pleasure spread over her face.

Jenna and Kate laughed.

"It looks like you're eating special restaurant food instead of soggy bread," Jenna said.

"What!" Mother looked hurt. She popped another bite into her mouth and let it melt away. "This is the world's greatest delicacy. Just try it."

"It looks like something we shouldn't miss, Jenna." Kate poured cream on her slice.

"This is your father's bread, Kate, and it's perfect," Mother said. "That's what gave me the idea of having cream on bread. Homemade bread is essential. Well, what do you think?"

Jenna took a bite and shivered. "It's soggy all right. I think I'll stick with peanut butter and jelly."

Kate had almost finished her slice. "I like it. It's a good treat."

Mother looked pleased. "That was our standard after-school snack."

"More than thirty years ago," Jenna added. "It was even before they invented McDonald's hamburgers."

"But not quite." Mother laughed. "For you two, that must seem like a long time ago." She fixed herself another slice. "It isn't just the taste, you know. Cream on bread is so full of memories. Here, Kate. Help yourself."

"No, thanks," Kate said politely.

"Mother has to eat a lot of it, so she can remember a story to tell us," Jenna said.

"That was delicious!" Mother said, when she was through. "And the memories are turning into a story. Let's move to the family room."

Kate slipped off her stool before anyone else could move. She put the cream in the refrigerator and stacked the dishes as though she were at her own house. Jenna picked up the forks and wiped off the counter. Mother looked surprised to see everything done so fast.

They settled comfortably on the couch.

"My story takes place on a summer Sunday when I was . . ." She stopped and looked at Jenna and Kate for a while. "I was a bit younger than you two. Maybe seven or eight."

"What was the sky like?" Jenna asked. "The sky is an important clue in Mom's stories," she explained to Kate.

Mother began again.

It was a clear, sunny afternoon. Only a long, knife-shaped cloud divided the sky above the children who gathered to play.

The children were four of my brothers, Harlan, Philip, Keith, and David, my sister Helene, and two neighbor boys, Jerry and Sonny Elseth. I was there too, of course. The younger children in our family were in the house with my parents, taking afternoon naps.

Since it was Sunday, farm work and most housework were at a standstill, and a bunch of active children were looking for fun. It was especially important to do something exciting to entertain and impress the neighbor boys.

"Let's climb the tallest pine tree, all the way to the top," Harlan suggested.

"No," Philip said. "You broke the top off last time you climbed it, so it isn't the tallest anymore. Let's hypnotize a chicken instead." He was talking about catching a chicken, putting her head under a wing, and gently rocking her for a few minutes. When the hen was set on the ground, she would put on a stumbly-bumbly show for her audience. All of a sudden, she would realize she was making a great fool of herself. She'd spread her wings and protest with loud squawks as she escaped from her laughing captors.

"Oh no," Keith said. "That was your idea last time, but I was the one who got in trouble for doing it."

"And Mamma says it's cruel," I reminded him.

"Anyway, I have a better idea," Keith continued. "It's something fun for all of us, even Jerry and Sonny."

"Can I do it?" Helene asked.

"Naw, it's only for big kids." Keith answered. "But you can watch."

"I'll do it," said David.

Whatever it was, I knew I'd do it. I was certainly one of the big kids.

"It'll be a contest," Keith explained, leading us to the woodshed. He pointed at the roof of the big, old building that leaned against a grove of trees. "Let's see who dares to walk the farthest on the roof."

"Yeah, that's fun," Harlan agreed. "The first half of the roof is good and solid, but the last part, near the hole, is rotten. Just be sure to walk along the nail heads. Then you know there are strong beams below."

Everyone climbed a tree on the solid end to get to the woodshed roof. We decided to take turns, in order of age. Harlan would go first, then Jerry, Sonny, Philip, Keith, I, and David would each follow. Helene would watch.

Harlan walked at a normal pace along the path of nails until he got about a yard from the hole, indicating the danger area. Then he held out his arms for balance. Heel to toe he moved slowly forward. We watched him stop and look down through the hole.

On the sod floor below, he could see a bent up washtub. I knew, because I had often stood by the washtub and looked up through that very hole, all the way to the sky.

Harlan looked like he was frozen to the spot. Then we heard him say softly, as though louder words would throw him off balance, "I think this is as far as anyone should go."

After all, he was the oldest and responsible for the safety of those who would come after him. We watched him turn around slowly and carefully, knowing that a misstep could throw him into rotten boards. He took a few careful steps, then continued quickly along the nail path toward us.

Keith whispered to me, "Harlan doesn't want anyone to go past his spot. That way he'll be the winner for sure." I knew Keith would go farther, and I always tried to go as far as he did.

Jerry, Sonny, and Philip all stopped short of Harlan's mark.

Keith started out confidently, sure to win. He hardly slowed down until he reached the hole. Only then did he use his arms to balance. He edged forward until he had passed Harlan's spot by about a foot. He turned around carefully and came back with a smug look on his face.

"The winner!" Harlan announced. Then he turned to Keith. "But you shouldn't have gone that far. It's too dangerous."

"Wait a minute," I said. "No one's the winner yet."

Everybody laughed, and I started out. Like Keith, I walked to the hole without stopping. Then I looked down. The washtub seemed far away. I wondered if I could turn around. It didn't matter. That problem I'd face later. My eyes focused on the winning destination. I stuck out my arms and put one foot in front of the other, wobbling like a hypnotized chicken. Finally, I passed Keith's spot. I was the winner! I might never get back, but I was the winner!

Faintly, I heard Harlan's voice. "Stay there. I'll get you from the other end."

He was right. I couldn't turn around. I glanced down and felt dizziness pull me toward the hole. Then I lost my balance. I grabbed frantically, but the rotten wood gave way. Downward I hurled and crashed onto the washtub.

Harlan was there almost immediately to help me up. My left hand hung limp from the wrist. I walked toward the house with the helpless hand resting like an injured bird on my good arm. An entourage of fellow contestants surrounded me.

My mother calmly made a dish towel into a sling, as she had done before for other broken limbs. She said good-bye and sent me out the door.

Father helped me into our '41 Ford, and we were off to the clinic. I remember nothing about being put to sleep and having my arm set.

What I remember vividly is that when I got home, a houseful of admiring brothers and sisters awaited me.

Harlan stood by my chair and announced, "Marie is the winner!" He tapped my cast with his fingernails. "And she's wearing her trophy."

"That's a great story, Mom!" Jenna felt a bit jealous. "You had so much fun when you were little, and you were so brave."

Kate nodded. "But didn't it hurt a lot, and weren't your parents mad at you?"

Mother stood up. "I suppose. But I liked the attention, and I loved being a winner. Now, how would you two like to go to Jenna's room and play with dolls?"

Not dolls, thought Jenna. I've got new things to do with Kate. Soon Mother won't be the only one with exciting stories to tell.

11

A Plan

Kate stopped at the door to Jenna's bed-room. "How beautiful! White furniture and roses growing on your curtains and even a canopy bed. You must just love it in here."

Jenna hadn't thought much about her room before. But she tried to see it through Kate's eyes. "I guess it *is* nice. Sleeping bags and trunks are more fun, though."

"Trade you!" Kate said. They both laughed.

"Come on," Jenna said. "I've got something to show you in the basement."

"Don't mess up the boxes," Mother called after them as they ran down the basement stairs.

"Look!" Jenna pulled a rope out from behind a packing crate. "You've got to help me tie this up on one of the ceiling boards, so I can practice swinging."

"Good!" Kate patted Jenna on the back. "You've got the rope-swinging fever too."

They found a spot where a short board was connected from the ceiling to a post in the unfinished basement.

"We can reach this board with a chair," Kate said.

Jenna dragged over an old chair. Kate climbed up and double tied the rope to the board. "I'll test it out for you," she said. "If it isn't strong enough, we'll find a ladder and tie the rope to one of the beams."

Kate moved the chair and walked backward holding the rope. She gave a little jump onto the rope. Immediately, she tumbled to the floor with the board clattering after her.

"Are you all right?" Jenna's hands shook as she helped Kate up. She hoped Mother hadn't heard the noise.

Kate rubbed one knee. "I'm okay. Just a little too heavy for that board."

Mother rushed down the stairs. "What's going on here?" She picked up the board with the rope hanging from it, then looked at the girls. "What on earth are you trying to do? Tear down the house and kill yourselves?"

Jenna felt guilty and embarrassed. "No," she said. "We were just having fun."

Kate untied the rope and laid it and the board on the chair. "My dad can nail the board back. It won't be hard."

"We'll take care of it," Mother said brusquely. She turned away from them with a frown. "Play upstairs now, until Mrs. Bradner comes."

Jenna and Kate sat together on the pink carpeting in Jenna's room, leaning against the rose-covered bedspread.

"Thanks for helping me, Kate. At least we know that doesn't work." Jenna giggled nervously. "I'm sorry about my mom. She gets kind of upset if she thinks I'm doing anything dangerous."

"I noticed," Kate said. "It kind of surprised me after that story and all."

Jenna thought for a while. "I think I know how to cure her from worrying about me. And I'm determined to do it!"

"Tell me!" Kate sounded curious and excited.

Jenna shivered with excitement. "I'm going to practice until I can swing from upstairs in your barn to the hay pile. *Then* I'll surprise Mom. When she sees that I'm as brave as she was, she'll let me do more things."

"Good plan!" Kate held out her palms, and Jenna slapped them.

When Mother tucked Jenna in for the night, she said, "That Kate is a real whirlwind, isn't she!"

"Don't you like her?" Jenna asked.

"I'm just not used to her. She's so different from Kari. And you're different when you're with her."

Jenna smiled. "I know. I like the way I am when I'm with Kate."

Practicing

enna called Kari on Sunday as they had planned. She told her about Kate, but not about the rope swinging. Kari told her about a new friend, another girl who liked to play games of let's pretend. Jenna and Kari decided they would visit each other next summer.

Monday finally came, and Jenna hurried to school. At noon, she and Kate would start making plans for Thursday, when she would go to the farm again.

Jenna read the story in her reading book about

Aurora and her father in Norway. The father reminded Jenna of Kate's father. Both of them stayed home to do housework while the mothers were away at work. It seemed so cozy to have a dad around to cook dinner and read stories and talk about problems. Jenna missed her dad a little, but he had always been too busy with office work to spend much time with her.

In math class, Mr. Larson had groups take turns going to the blackboard to work out problems. Jenna sat at her desk and watched Kate and Buzz do their work next to each other. Shivers ran down her arms when Buzz made his chalk screech. Jenna wondered how Buzz would try to bug Kate today. He was too chicken to bother her on the playground anymore, so now he tried to get her into trouble in school.

Suddenly, Buzz reached over and grabbed Kate's chalk away from her. He went back to work as though nothing had happened. Kate eyed him for a moment, then quickly reached for her chalk. Buzz let it drop to the floor and whined loudly, "Kate, you broke my chalk."

Mr. Larson's stern voice interrupted. "Kate

and Buzz, report back to the room instead of to the playground after lunch."

Jenna was disappointed. Buzz could get into trouble if he wanted to, but he could just leave Kate alone.

"Sorry you have to stay in," she told Kate in the cafeteria.

Kate shrugged. "I'm used to it. Dad says I'm too impulsive. I do things before I think. But I've been trying to do better in this new school."

"Maybe we can help each other," Jenna said. "You can teach *me* to be more impulsive, and I'll help you be less impulsive."

"Your mother wouldn't be very happy if you turned into a troublemaker." Kate looked serious. "Maybe she'd blame me."

Jenna felt bad that Kate even thought such a thing. "My mom will really like you when she gets to know you better."

They emptied their trays. "See you later," Jenna said.

Kate waved and walked toward the classroom.

Jenna stood at the edge of the playground for a minute and then decided to play dodge. She had to have lots of exercise to be ready for Thursday. It was the first time she had played without Kate, so she felt a little shy about joining the group. But the other kids moved over to make room for her in the lineup. It made her feel good to belong.

Before the end of the hour, Kate joined them too. Jenna saw Buzz leaning against the school wall alone, watching the game. She felt sorry for him. Buzz was more alone than she would ever be. He didn't even know how to be friendly.

"What happened?" she asked Kate as they walked back to school. "Did Mr. Larson scold you?"

Kate shook her head. "He talked to me a little before Buzz got to the room. He said he wanted me to understand that Buzz is having a hard time both at school and at home. And I told him that's what I figured."

Jenna felt proud of Kate. She knew Kate was helping her understand people too.

Kate continued. "When Buzz came in, Mr. Larson had us put up a Halloween bulletin board together."

"What did Buzz say to you?"

"Just, 'I hate girls.' "

Jenna and Kate laughed.

"But I think he really liked doing the bulletin board," Kate said. "I made a witch stand on her head on his jack-o'-lantern." Jenna giggled. "Buzz looked like he was mad, but he found a black cat and put it upside down on my ghost. When I laughed, he tried to hide his smile, but I saw it."

"I suppose you're going to be playing with Buzz instead of me from now on," Jenna teased.

"Sure," Kate said. "And I'll teach him to rope swing before you."

"Oh no! You are looking at the soon-to-be champion of the hayloft." Jenna announced dramatically.

As Jenna had hoped, Mother wasn't there yet when she got home from school.

She didn't even stop for a snack but hurried downstairs. It was all planned out. She carried the stepladder to the spot where there was a space above a ceiling beam, grabbed the rope, and climbed up. She pushed the rope end into the space, pulled it through, and knotted it several times. Then she scattered the old sofa cushions on the floor.

Great! Jenna was all set for the test swing. She carried the rope in the opposite direction from the cushions, reached high on the rope, wrapped her fingers tightly around it, and lifted her feet from the floor. A second later, she dropped onto the cushions. It was a fast ride, but it worked.

Swing and drop and walk. Soon Jenna's arms were too tired and weak for even one more swing. She climbed the ladder and hid the rope in the space between the ceiling and beam. Then she put the ladder away and rearranged the cushions. Wouldn't Mother be surprised!

On Tuesday, her arms were so sore that it was hard to get started, but she was determined to practice anyway. After a few minutes, the soreness eased and she forgot about it.

On Wednesday, Jenna practiced swinging back and forth as many times as possible without dropping. She wrapped her legs tightly around the rope to lessen the weight on her arms.

Back and forth. Back and forth. Jenna strained every muscle in her body to hold on for one more round. Back and forth.

Ten times! She was ready.

Jenna's Story

Jenna stepped out of the house in her raincoat Thursday morning. A chilly rain was falling from dark clouds.

Jenna pushed Mother's "Be careful!" to the back of her mind. She had listened to Mother's stories for as long as she could remember. She had read hundreds of other people's stories. And she had imagined stories with Kari. Today she would live her own story. And tomorrow night, with Kate as her witness, *she* would be the story-teller.

The school day seemed endless. It was hard to concentrate on equivalent fractions, and the steppes of Russia, and the skeletal system of bones with funny names like "ulna" and "fibula."

Finally, Mr. Larson said, "Clear off your desks and get your coats—*quietly*."

Jenna jumped up and bumped her desk. Her school box fell to the floor. Markers and pencils rolled everywhere. Oh no. Wouldn't she ever get to that swinging rope!

It was hard to pick up markers quickly in the midst of moving feet. She just couldn't miss the bus.

"Get your jacket," Kate's voice interrupted. "I'll pick these up."

Finally Jenna was hurrying toward the bus. "I didn't think this day would ever be over." Jenna panted as she tried to keep up with Kate.

"It sounds like you have big plans," Kate said.

Yes, she had a great plan! Jenna bounded up the steps.

Just as Jenna sat down by Mara, Buzz got on

the bus. He pointed at Jenna. But before he could say anything about her clumsiness, Jenna smiled and said, "Hi, Buzz!"

His hand dropped, and he hurried toward the backseat.

"You surprised him," Mara said. "He's so mean that he isn't used to people being nice to him."

"I surprised myself too," Jenna said. "I guess I'm learning to be impulsive like Kate."

Kate gestured toward Tommy's seat. "Tommy's doing okay too. He said Buzz didn't bother him when I wasn't on the bus last Friday."

"That's because he sat by me," Mara said. "*Nobody* dares to bother me."

"Better not let Tommy hear you say that," Kate warned. The three girls laughed.

Jenna concentrated on trees moving past the windows. She swung like Tarzan from each one.

"What are you doing, Jenna?" Mara asked.

Embarrassed, Jenna realized she was holding out tense fists. She let her hands fall into her lap. "I guess I'm still practicing rope swinging."

"What step are you going to practice from today?" Kate asked.

"None!" She wondered what Kate would think about her secret.

"What do you mean?" Kate sounded a bit worried.

"I hung the rope on a strong beam, and I've been practicing every day." She proudly showed them her hands, covered with red patches and dried skin that had been blisters. "I can swing ten times in a row."

"You'll soon be ready then," Kate said. "How about if you practice from the top steps today. And next Thursday you can take the big swing."

"But, Kate, I'm ready now! I've been waiting all week for this."

Molly, Seetuk, Panther, and Dusty were huddled together under an umbrella, waiting for the bus.

Jenna shivered as she stepped into the drizzle and wind. "Hi, Molly," she called out. She didn't have time to pet the animals right now.

She headed straight for the barn. "I'm not

hungry," she called out. She had to get to the hayloft before she lost her nerve.

"Tell Dad we'll be there in a little while," Kate called to Mara and Molly. She caught up with Jenna.

Tommy ran past them. "I get to swing first!" he shouted, dropping his book bag and jacket in a corner.

Jenna watched every move Tommy made. He did a double swing. It looked easy. Why did she feel so scared? She gritted her teeth. If she didn't climb the ladder now, she'd never do it.

"My turn!" she announced. Without giving Kate a chance to stop her, she ran toward the ladder.

The rope felt a lot thicker than the one in the basement. For a moment she hesitated. But if Mara could hang on with *her* little hands, she could too. She didn't dare look down at Kate. This was her big moment.

Jenna held her breath and swung out.

The hay pile appeared too soon. The rope swung back. She hadn't let go! Panic tightened her body. The open space appeared again. It was a long drop down.

She tried to kick the ledge to swing back, the way Tommy had. But her foot brushed the ledge and dangled in the air. She couldn't get the leg back to the rope.

Her arms felt like they were ripping out at the sockets. Her slipping hands burned. She tried to tighten her grip, but the rope tore at her fingers.

The deep hole opened below. Her body broke loose and plunged downward. Her arms shot out to break the fall. She crumpled to the ground.

Pain shot through her body. Something kept on hurting. At least she could move.

With one arm, she pushed herself to a sitting position. She tried to lift the other arm. It didn't work. Her right arm just hung at her side. It didn't seem to be a part of her. But the throbbing ache reminded her that it was. Tears blurred her eyes. What should she do?

"Tommy, run and get Dad!" Kate's urgent words made Jenna feel a little better. Kate and her dad would know what to do.

"Oh, Jenna." Kate knelt by her and put an arm around her back. "Can you get up?"

"It's my arm. I don't think I need it to walk with." Jenna tried to laugh, but it sounded like a sob.

Kate helped her to her feet. Jenna carried the limp arm in her other hand. A picture of her mother doing the same thing flashed through her mind.

Jenna was surprised to see that the rain had stopped, and the sun was peeking out from behind a white cloud. If this were a story, the sky would be black.

Mr. Bradner ran out of the house to meet them. He looked at Jenna's arm. "It doesn't take an X ray to tell us that's a broken arm. Kate, go to the house and get a towel. Jenna, I'll help you into the pickup, and we'll head for the hospital. We'll have to call your mother from there."

When Kate brought the towel, her father folded it, gently slipped Jenna's arm into it, and tied it at the back of her neck. It felt good to have the sore arm supported by the sling.

"Take care of the children, Kate," Mr. Bradner said. "Mother will soon be here."

Tommy and Mara and Molly stood in a row

and waved. Kate held Dusty up to the pickup window. Jenna smiled on the outside. Inside, she felt as if she were still hanging over a dark hollow. She had never been to a hospital before.

Jenna kept her head turned toward the window, so Mr. Bradner wouldn't see the tears roll from her cheeks onto the dish towel sling. This hadn't turned out the right way at all. By now she was supposed to be able to tell a story about how brave she was. She might as well get used to it; she just wasn't made like Mother and Kate. She was scared stiff from head to toe—petrified.

Brave

Mr. Bradner opened the Emergency Department door and guided Jenna to a waiting room chair. "I'll talk to the receptionist and call your mother."

Soon Mr. Bradner sat down in the chair next to Jenna. "I left a message for your mother. While we're waiting for her, you'll have some X rays taken. Then the doctor will talk to you so you'll know what to expect."

"What *will* happen next?" Jenna could feel

her lip tremble. The lump in her stomach hurt worse than the arm.

Mr. Bradner smiled and patted Jenna's good arm. "I can tell you that, because I broke an ankle a couple years ago. I remember how scared I was."

Jenna was surprised. Mr. Bradner had been scared?

"The doctor will explain to you what needs to be done to straighten out your arm," Mr. Bradner continued. "You may be either asleep or awake for that, depending on how the X rays look. A cast will be put on to hold the bones straight while they heal. Then the fun begins! Your friends get to autograph your cast. And I'm going to wait right here to be first—if you'll let me. How's that?"

Jenna nodded. She just wished Mother would come.

"Jenna Wexler to X ray," a voice announced.

She followed a man in a white jacket. "Hi, Jenna. I'm Scott. Some people call me an X-ray technologist, but I just think of myself as a bone photographer. Sit down on this rolling stool."

He slipped her arm out of the sling and placed it carefully on a framed cardboard. "The film is in this cassette," he explained.

He laid a long sandbag across her hand. "That's so you don't try to wave." He stepped out of the room and called out his instructions, "Tell your bones to say, 'Cheese!' " Jenna smiled to herself. She almost forgot that it hurt to hold her arm flat.

In a few minutes, the X rays were developed. "Your bones have a beautiful but crooked smile," Scott told Jenna. "Just follow this nurse to an examining room where you'll meet the bone doctor."

Jenna was glad to find Kate's father waiting for her. While she was telling him about the funny bone photographer, a woman wearing a long, white coat hurried into the office.

"Hi, I'm Dr. Newland." She gave Jenna's left hand a reassuring squeeze. Then she gently examined the broken arm. "Mr. Bradner tells me you're practicing to be a hayloft acrobat."

"Well, I was," Jenna said, knowing this was the end of rope swinging for her. She wasn't sure whether she was relieved or disappointed about that.

Dr. Newland took a large folder from the desk and pulled out a black sheet. "Let's take a look at your X rays on the view box." She hung the sheet on a box and switched on a light. It seemed strange to Jenna that this was really a picture of her. The bones in her science book had seemed so unreal, like Halloween decorations. But these were hers and very real!

"Just as I thought," Dr. Newland said. "Both the radius and the ulna are broken." She showed Jenna. "See, these two bones should be straight. Instead, about halfway between the wrist and the elbow, they form angles. In medical language, we say they're angulated."

Jenna nodded. Now she knew what the X-ray technologist meant by a crooked smile.

The doctor switched off the light. "I'll straighten out the angles, and your bones should heal nicely."

She sat down facing Jenna. "Fortunately, your break is not complicated, and the bones can be set quickly. So you have a decision to make. I could manipulate your arm to set it right here in the office. It's painful but takes only a few seconds. Or you could go to an operating room where you would be put to sleep before I set your arm. You wouldn't feel the pain, but you would have to stay here for a few hours. Which do you think would be better for you?"

Panic gripped Jenna. What did *she* think! She had never made a big decision like this before. She didn't know how to decide. Mr. Bradner was watching her, but he didn't make any suggestions. Mother had always made the decisions about whether she should take cough syrup or go to the doctor or stay home from school with a cold. "My mother will be here soon," she said softly.

"It is best for you to make this decision," Dr. Newland said. "Then when your mother comes, she can sign the necessary papers, and I'll be ready to do the job."

Jenna tried to think. She wished she wouldn't have to feel the pain when the doctor fixed her arm. But she wanted to go home as soon as possible. So far, she had been able to stand the hurting. Her determination started to come back. It was the same feeling she'd had when she decided to swing on the rope. And it was the feeling she had when she said "Hi" to Buzz. She made the decision herself.

She tried to smile. "I want to be awake."

Dr. Newland smiled back. "Good. I thought you'd be a brave one. As soon as your mother comes, I'll show you how to set an arm."

After she left the room, Mr. Bradner said, "That was a very brave decision, Jenna."

Brave. No one had ever called her brave before. And now she had heard it twice. She liked it.

"It's going to take a few weeks to get that arm healed up," Mr. Bradner said. "By that time, I'll be sure to have a good pile of hay covering the spot where you fell. And I'll be there to watch you, just in case you decide to make an other trip into space."

"That means I have another decision to make," Jenna said.

Just then Mother rushed into the room. Her lips trembled on Jenna's cheek. "I'm so sorry, honey."

Jenna was surprised that Mother seemed upset. She had sounded so heroic when she told about breaking her own arm.

Dr. Newland came back in. "Would you like to stay, Mrs. Wexler?"

A strange look crossed Mother's face. "No, I'll be in the waiting room." She gave Jenna a quick hug and left with Mr. Bradner.

Dr. Newland helped Jenna onto the examining table. She put her hands firmly around Jenna's arm. "I'm going to put my thumbs together, Jenna, and push against the angle. This is going to hurt, but it will be over quickly. Are you ready?"

Before Jenna could nod, she felt a sharp pain in her arm. Then it was over. Tears ran down the sides of her face and into her ears.

"You did just fine," Dr. Newland said. "Now all we have left is the cast."

A nurse set a bucket of water on a stool and opened some little packages.

"First we'll put a fingerless stocking on your hand," Dr. Newland explained, as she worked. Next she wrapped a fluffy gauze around Jenna's arm. Then she took a dripping roll of wet bandage the nurse handed her. "This is the plaster.

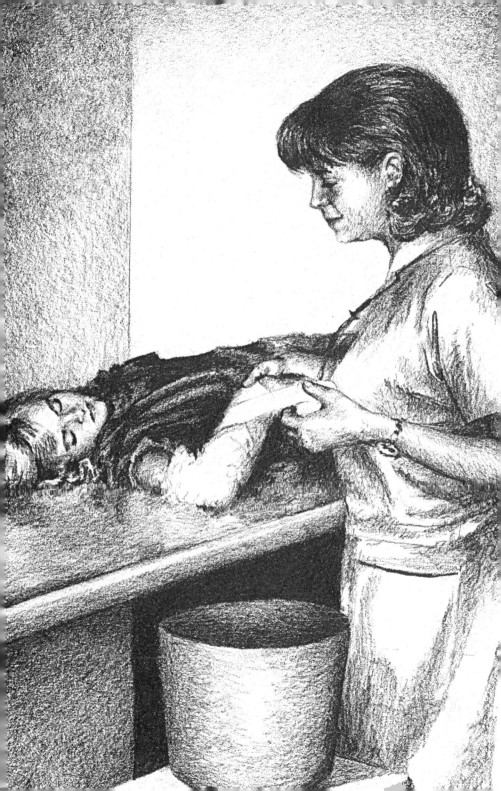

It will dry solid to hold your arm straight." She wrapped the plaster from Jenna's hand to above her elbow.

"It feels so good," Jenna said. The warm moisture soothed and relaxed her sore arm.

Jenna's attention turned to a picture on the wall. It was of a little kitten with a splint on the right foreleg. Big eyes begged Jenna to give the kitten a home. What a great idea! They could heal up together.

"Now that's what I call a good patient!" Dr. Newland patted the plaster and folded the stocking over the edge of the cast in Jenna's palm. "Be sure to put a plastic bag over the cast when you bathe, so it doesn't soften up. And come back to visit me in two weeks."

Jenna met Mother and Mr. Bradner in the waiting room. "Dr. Newland was so nice, and she taught me how to put on a cast."

Mr. Bradner laughed. "I suppose you liked it so much that you'll want to come back often."

Mother didn't seem to think that was very funny.

"Oh, I can't forget the autograph party." Mr. Bradner took out his pen and signed, "Jon B."

He smiled at Jenna. "You and I know that *B* doesn't stand only for Bradner."

Jenna nodded proudly. "Thanks! Tell Kate I'll see her soon."

On the way home, Jenna waited for Mother to say something. But she was quiet, so Jenna talked. "Don't worry about it happening again, Mom. Mr. Bradner said he'd put a pile of hay on the ground where I fell."

"No!" Mother interrupted sharply. "It won't happen again, because you won't do such a dangerous thing again."

Jenna's good feelings drained out of her.

Desperate words tumbled out of her mouth. "You remember the stories. But you don't remember what it *feels* like to be a child." She had to make Mother understand. "Don't you know that I have to live my own stories?"

Her arm was heavy. Tears rushed down her cheeks, and she was too tired to hold back the sobs any longer.

A New Story

A rope dangled in front of Jenna, but when she tried to grab it, it moved away into darkness. She lost her balance and screamed.

A firm hand cooled her forehead, and Jenna sank back into soft hay.

Darkness soon returned, and her arms became heavy. Sweaty hands were slipping, slipping, slipping. She held on tightly but kept on falling, falling, falling. Someone was moaning and groaning.

A cool washcloth wiped her hands and face,

and Jenna tried to wake up. But she had to go back to the hayloft to tie a knot on the end of the rope.

Back and forth, back and forth, back and forth she swung. The rope wouldn't stop. She was getting dizzy. She had to jump off. But the space beneath her was dark and deep. She cried out for help!

Strong arms caught her, and a gentle voice said, "I am here with you." The sound soothed Jenna, and she fell into a deep, peaceful sleep.

When she woke up, she was glad it was light. She lay still and watched sunshine dance with the curtain roses. She thought about yesterday. And she made plans for the new day.

Mother peeked into the room and smiled. "You're finally awake."

"What day is it?" Jenna asked.

"It's Friday morning. Almost nine o'clock."

"You mean that was only one night. I had enough nightmares for a whole week."

Mother brushed the hair off Jenna's forehead and sat down on a chair beside the bed. "Yes, it was a long night. You hallucinated. And I had a lot of time to think."

"What did you think about?"

"About what you said last night, and . . ."

"I'm sorry," Jenna interrupted. "I was just tired and upset."

"Yes, I know. But you said some important things." Mother centered Jenna's casted arm comfortably on a little pillow. "I may have forgotten some of my childhood feelings, but I can tell you *someone* I'm just beginning to understand."

"Who's that?" Jenna wondered.

"My own mother, Grandma Paulsen. Last night I thought about all the broken bones and stitches and tonsillectomies of eleven children." Mother shook her head and sighed. "I'm amazed that she lived through those years."

"And you're having a hard time with one child," Jenna teased. "What else did you think about?"

"I realized that my exciting stories aren't a very accurate picture of my childhood. I remembered that it wasn't always fun to be Marie Paulsen. I was usually working hard to compete with my brothers, and . . ."

"And you were impulsive."

"How did you know?"

"And you sometimes had to stay in your classroom at noon hour."

Mother looked puzzled. "I never told you about that."

Jenna smiled mysteriously. "I just guessed." She wondered how long it would take Mother to notice that Kate was a lot like her.

Suddenly Jenna remembered it was Friday. "But, Mom. Don't you have to go to work?"

"No, you and I are taking the day off to do what you like."

"Really!" Jenna knew just what she'd like to do. "How about if we start by making up a new story—together."

"Fine. How does it start?" Mother asked.

"It starts with the sky, of course. And you have to listen carefully, because it's a clue to the rest of the story."

"I'm listening."

Jenna began. "The sky is a white cushion of clouds. Peeking over the edge of the cushion is a very lonely, very fluffy kitten. On the ground below stands a girl with an arm in a cast. But both arms are stretched out, waiting to cuddle that lonely kitten." Jenna stopped. "Now it's your turn, Mom."

"I think I'm being tricked into something," Mother said. She thought for a while, then continued the story.

"A gullible mother drives two girls—one with a cast on her arm and the other, her friend with laughing eyes—to the Humane Society. Soon the girl with a cast holds a fluffy kitten. Happy tears blur the girl's eyes, but a small, sandpapery tongue tickles her neck and makes her laugh."

Mother smiled at Jenna. "Is that what it feels like to be a child?"

Jenna gave Mother a one-armed hug. In her dramatic voice, she said, "Yes, there is evidence to indicate that you are beginning to remember."

They laughed together and got ready to live the new story.